Thomas Corwin Mendenhall

The Alaskan Boundary Line

Thomas Corwin Mendenhall

The Alaskan Boundary Line

ISBN/EAN: 9783742810113

Manufactured in Europe, USA, Canada, Australia, Japa

Cover: Foto ©Andreas Hilbeck / pixelio.de

Manufactured and distributed by brebook publishing software
(www.brebook.com)

Thomas Corwin Mendenhall

The Alaskan Boundary Line

T H E

A L A S K A   B O U N D A R Y   L I N E

BY

THOMAS CORWIN MENDENHALL

FROM

THE INDEPENDENT

OCTOBER 26 1899

A Ballad of Hallowmass.

By Clinton Scollard.

IT happed at the time of Hallowmass, when the dead may walk abroad,
That the wraith of Ralph of the peaceful heart went forth from the courts of God.
Went forth from the paradisial ways, from the paths of asphodel,
From the vistas veiled in a golden haze where the souls of the sainted dwell;
And as he passed he heard the peal of the summoning trumpet blown,
And he saw the cloud of witnesses go wavering by to the throne;
And earthward swift on a tide of joy and love he seemed to swim,
For he thought of the hour when his stalwart sons should go to the throne with him;
When they should stand on his either hand who had been his pride on earth,
And know in the sight of the Living Light the bliss of a second birth.

And so to the land he had called his own, to the realm he had ruled, he came,
Where, under the spell of his gracious sway, grim war had been but a name,
Where the herds had strayed on the happy hills, and traffic roared in the mart,
Where life had lost its cankering ills, for peace had flowered in the heart.
But lo ! as he looked on the harvest fields, on the ways of the wide-wheeled wain,
He saw wild masses of marching men sweep over the pillaged plain;
He saw no flocks on the great green slopes, no kine in barn or byre,
But the sheltering thatch of the farmstead roof licked up by the tongues of fire;
And the women's groans and the children's moans surged by him like a wave,
And the cloudy reek of plundered towns where none was left to save.
Then on he pressed to the seat of power in the crook of a broad sea bay,
Where, under the frown of the bastioned walls, the lines of a leaguer lay;
In he went to the tallest tent, and sat unseen at the board
Where the fierce chiefs plotted the city's sack, each chief with his barèd sword;
He who sat at the council's head was the leaguer's grimmest one,
And the dead King looked in his fiery eyes and knew the man for his son.
So forth he went from the tallest tent, by the leaguer's outmost guard,
Till he came to the moat and the mighty keep and the archway triple-barred;
Not a warder's eye as he slipped by beheld the wraith of the King,
And scarce, as he sped toward the castle gate, did he meet with a living thing,
For Famine into the weedy streets had come as a grizzly guest,
And down from the pallid window-panes there peered the face of the Pest.
He glided into the castle court, and on to the banquet-hall
Wherefrom there echoed a mirthful rouse in iterant rise and fall:
He looked within for a little space, then shrunk him back from the door,
For he saw the face of his other son and a painted paramour.

It happed at the time of Hallowmass, when the dead may walk abroad,
That the wraith of Ralph of the peaceful heart went back to the courts of God;
And a bitterer anguish than was his few noble souls have known
As he saw the cloud of witnesses go wavering down from the throne.
He passed to the high and holy place, and straight to the feet of Him
About whom stand in a shining band the saints and the seraphim:
" I pray," he said, " that my soul may tread the dark of the outer way,
That those I love may be borne above to the light of the living day;
Send thou my soul to the utmost goal of night to dwell therein,
That they thereby may be raised on high from the awful pits of sin ! "
But the Presence spake: " Remorse shall wake because of these words of thine
Within the breasts of the recreant ones ere another day decline;
And they shall win from the ways of sin, ere the span of their lives be through,
Because of the love of a father's heart, and the deed that thou wouldst do ! "
And so from the time of Hallowmass, when the dead may walk abroad,
The soul of Ralph of the peaceful heart abode in the courts of God.

CLINTON, N. Y.

The Alaska Boundary Line.

By T. C. Mendenhall,

PRESIDENT OF WORCESTER POLYTECHNIC INSTITUTE,

DISPUTES over boundary lines have always been most difficult of settlement. Most nations are reluctant to give up territory, even when it is apparently of little value, immediate or prospective. The United States has been more nearly an exception to this rule than any other great nation. This is undoubtedly owing to the enormous extent of our original possessions, considered in relation to our comparatively small population. Because our territory has been generally far in excess of the demands of our people we have been indifferent and careless as to the disposition of outlying regions which have not, for the time, seemed of much concern to our welfare. Most of our controversies have been with a nation whose policy is always the exact opposite of this; a nation which promptly seizes all that comes within its reach, and never gives up a foot. In all of our boundary disputes with Great Britain we have been worsted; that is, we have yielded territory to which our claim was as good as hers and often better. It is to be regretted that our people have not been generally well informed as to the merits of these controversies and, especially, that they have not felt a greater interest in the outcome. We have been so busy in the occupation and development of the great interior that a few hundred square miles here and there of distant, unsettled regions have not seemed to be important.

The boundary line between Alaska and British Columbia, now under discussion, is involved in peculiar difficulties. Its importance has greatly increased within the last two or three years on account of the discovery and development of rich mining resources in its neighborhood. It ought to have been fixed long ago, and might have been with vastly less irritation and friction than are now unavoidable.

The desirability of coming to an agreement with Great Britain was long ago recognized by all who were familiar with the facts, but one administration after another has found itself so occupied with other, generally much less important, affairs that it was easier to postpone than to act. In 1891 and 1892, in official communications relating to this and other public business, forwarded to the then Secretary of State, Mr. Blaine, the pressing importance of a determination of this line was urged, and these letters were forwarded by him in regular course to Congress, together with his approval of the suggestions they embodied. They received little attention. This was prior to the discoveries of gold in the Klondike region and there is no doubt that a settlement might then have been reached with comparatively little effort.

The difficulty is one which we inherited from Russia, and it arises primarily out of the unfortunate and ambiguous definition of the boundary found in the treaty between Russia and Great Britain in 1825. When we bought Alaska in 1867 we bought that definition and all of the trouble to which it must necessarily give rise. All nations ought to have learned long ago that *boundary lines should be defined astronomically.* The latitude and longitude of any point on the earth may now be determined with almost any desired degree of precision. Natural boundary marks, such as rivers and mountains, although apparently meeting every requirement, are far from satisfactory. Rivers change their courses; we have had disputes growing out of this fact, and we had a long controversy with Great Britain to determine which river *was* the St. Croix of the treaty. Mountains are erroneously named and often do not really exist as shown on an explorer's map. Much of the trouble over the Alaskan boundary has arisen out of confusions of this sort. English and American astronomers would never differ, sensibly, over the location of the 141st meridian.

Fortunately a large part of the Alaskan

boundary line is astronomical. It is that part which proceeds from a point near the summit of Mt. St. Elias along the 141st meridian west of Greenwich to the Arctic Ocean. Over this there is no dispute, or if a dispute should ever arise it can easily be settled. The line separating what is known as Southeast Alaska from British Columbia, beginning at the most southerly point of Prince of Wales Island and ending near the summit of Mt. St. Elias, is the subject of the present controversy.

The language of the treaty is as follows: " Commencing from the southernmost point of the island called Prince of Wales Island, which point lies in the parallel of 54° 41' north latitude, and between the 131st and 133d degree of west longitude (meridian of. Greenwich),the said line shall ascend to the north along the channel called Portland Channel as far as the point of the continent where it strikes the 56th degree of north latitude; from this last mentioned point the line of demarcation shall follow the summit of the mountains situated parallel to the coast as far as the point of intersection of the 141st degree of west longitude (of the same meridian, and finally, from the said point of intersection, the said meridian line of the 141st degree, in its prolongation as far as the Frozen Ocean."

The first serious difficulty is to determine what is meant by " the channel called Portland Channel." Our friends the enemy interpret this to mean that on leaving the southernmost point of Prince of Wales Island the line must be drawn at once to the north to the 56th parallel of north latitude, and this carries it to the west of the great Revilla Gigedo Island into Burrough's Bay. thus throwing that island and a large block of the mainland under their jurisdiction. In order to enter what has always been known as Portland Channel it is necessary to proceed from the beginning at Prince of Wales Island straight to the east for about sixty miles, and then " ascend to the north along the channel," which is the line we claim. The omission of this easterly line from the treaty opens the door for the British contention, and to support it they maintain that the use of the name Portland Channel was an oversight. We contend, on the

contrary, that the omission of the fifty or sixty miles of easting from the southernmost point of Prince of Wales Island is of no special importance because any one would understand that before you could ascend along the channel you must get into it. On the 56th parallel, therefore, the two claims are separated by the distance from Burrough's Bay to the head of Portland Channel, a matter of about thirty-five miles. From this point until they come together near Mt. St. Elias they continue to be apart by about the same distance. Roughly, then, there is in dispute an irregular strip of territory about 700 miles long, with an average width of 35 to 40 miles, nearly three and a half times the area of the State of Massachusetts. The line contended for by the British follows the shore from Burrough's Bay to the mouth of the Stikine River, thence, still as close to the shore as it can be shown upon an ordinary map, to the Taku Inlet, which it crosses at the southern end and then, turning to the west, it crosses Lynn Canal, leaving all of that splendid estuary on the Canadian side, likewise the wonderful Glacier Bay, with its famous Muir Glacier, going straight for the Fairweather Mountains, which it follows to Mt. St. Elias. This claim is based on the next phrase of the treaty, which declares that after leaving Portland Channel " the line of demarcation shall follow the summit of the mountains situated parallel to the coast as far as the point of intersection of the 141st degree of west longitude, etc." On the old chart by Vancouver on which the treaty was based, a range of mountains parallel to the coast and situated about thirty-five miles back from the shore is shown, the summits being beautifully arranged in a continuous chain. Undoubtedly such a range was supposed to exist at that time, but the English diplomats who framed the treaty with Russia evidently suspected that its position might not be shown correctly on Vancouver's map, and fearing that it was really further inland than it there appeared they thought it wise to insert a modifying clause by which Russia could be prevented from getting too wide a strip of the western coast. The nearer the supposed range of mountains was to the shore line the better for them, so they did not propose to limit its position on that side, but lest it should stray too far to the east they shrewdly provided as follows: "That whenever the summit of the mountains which extend in a direction parallel to the coast from the 56th degree of north latitude to the point of intersection of the 141st degree of west longitude shall prove to be at the distance of more than ten marine leagues from the ocean, the limit between the British possessions and the line of coast which is to belong to Russia, as above mentioned (that is to say, the limit of the possessions ceded by this convention) shall be formed by a line parallel to the winding of the coast, and which shall never exceed the distance of ten marine leagues therefrom."

Now the American contention is that there is no such range of mountains parallel to the coast; mountains there are in plenty; Southeast Alaska is covered with them, but they are scattered about in absolute irregularity; generally increasing in hight toward the east, but nowhere simulating a "range" even approximately like that shown on Vancouver's chart. This being the case, it is contended that it is necessary to fall back upon the alternative definition of the line in which the *intent* of the language of the treaty is clearly that Russia should be possessed of a strip ten marine leagues (about thirty-five miles) in width, counting from the "winding of the coast." The line claimed by us is drawn upon this assumption. Mountains being extremely numerous all over this strip of territory, the English have no difficulty in drawing their line from peak to peak so that it shall practically follow the water's edge, and this, they claim, is following "the summit of the mountains situated parallel to the coast."

Of course there is much involved in this controversy besides the mere question of square miles of territory. The really serious object of Great Britain is to secure one or more seaports and access to the interior without coming under American jurisdiction, which means the breaking of the continuity of our coast line so that instead of controlling, practically, the entire western coast, except that part from Cape Flattery to 54° 40' north latitude, which we gave up to her in 1846, our jurisdiction as far as Mt. St. Elias will be over a series of disconnected

fragments. It will be seen from the above brief statement of the case that, considering the literal interpretation of the treaty as it stands, the affair is one of much perplexity, and that it is by no means one-sided. The phrase, "following the summit of the mountains situated parallel to the coast," is, it must be confessed, of uncertain meaning. It does not say the *range* of mountains parallel to the coast. If it did the meaning would be clear, but on the other hand it may be fairly claimed that *range* is implied; otherwise there is the manifestly absurd assumption that mountains, or a mountain, may be situated parallel to the coast.

In the face of this ambiguity we may fall back upon a generally accepted principle in boundary disputes that continuous occupation of territory or undisputed recognition of a line shall have a determining effect. It cannot be denied that up to a comparatively recent date, about 1887, the line was drawn upon English maps essentially as upon those of Russia, or upon our own, and there is much evidence to show that this line was what was meant in the treaty. Before Alaska came into our possession there was a strong feeling among Canadians that this strip, now known as Southeast Alaska, ought to belong to Great Britain, but it was not held that it was hers in virtue of the treaty. In illustration of this I will make a few quotations from a prominent Canadian newspaper printed in 1863, shortly after the finding of gold in the sands of the Stikine River, a discovery which was thought at the time to be of much importance:

"It is certainly not acceptable . . . that the business of such a highway should reach the interior through a Russian door of thirty miles of coast. . . . It is clearly undesirable that the strip three hundred miles long and thirty miles wide, which is only used by the Russians for the collection of furs and walrus teeth, shall forever control the entrance to our very extensive northern territory. . . . The strip of land which stretches along from Portland Canal to Mt. St. Elias with a breadth of thirty miles and which, according to the treaty of 1825, forms a part of Russian America, must eventually become the property of Great Britain."

It is important to note in these extracts,

and many others similar in strain could be quoted, the admission of practically everything now claimed by us—the Portland Canal, the thirty miles width, and the fact that the treaty of 1825 made this the property of Russia.

Naturally the thing for the United States to do was to stand by this interpretation, so long accepted by the English, and to declare that the territory was ours. We shall be compelled, however, to allow the matter to go into arbitration. If arbitration means a decision in accord with the principles of justice and equity, we ought to welcome such a determination of the case. But in modern diplomacy arbitration means compromise, and we may as well resign ourselves to the cutting in two of our Alaskan domain and the rupture of the continuity of our coast line. We are driven to arbitration by our own act of a few years ago when we "thrust ourselves into a controversy over a boundary line on another continent, in which we can have no interest except, perhaps, that which grows out of a very foggy and uncertain sentiment." This result was distinctly foreseen more than three years ago, and predicted in an article printed in the *Atlantic Monthly* for April, 1896, the closing paragraph of which is as follows:

"The truth is that Great Britain is meeting our own wishes in this matter with almost indecent haste, because the arbitration of the Alaska boundary line, by which she hopes and expects to acquire an open sea coast for her great northwestern territories, and to weaken us by breaking our exclusive jurisdiction north of 54° 40', is enormously more important to her than anything she is likely to gain or lose in South America. Having driven her to accept arbitration in this case it will be impossible for us to refuse it in Alaska, and we shall find ourselves again badly worsted by the diplomatic skill of a people who, as individuals, have developed intellectual activity, manliness, courage, unselfish devotion to duty, and general nobility of character elsewhere unequaled in the world's history, but whose diplomatic policy as a nation is and long has been characterized by aggressiveness, greed, absolute indifference to the rights of others, and a splendid facility in ignoring every principle of justice or international law whenever commercial interests are at stake."

WORCESTER, MASS.

Notes of an Itinerant Policeman.*
II.—THE HABITUAL CRIMINAL.
By Josiah Flynt.

IN appearance and manner the professional offender has not changed much in the last decade. I knew him first over ten years ago when, making my earliest studies of tramp life, I saw him again five years ago while on a short trip in Hoboland, and we have met recently on the railroads; and he looks just about as he did when we first got acquainted.

Ordinarily he would not be noticed in mixed company by others than those accustomed to his ways. He is not like the tramp whom practically any one can pick out in a crowd. He dresses well, can often carry himself after the manner of a gentle-

man, and generally has a snug sum of money in his pockets. It is his face, voice and habits of companionship that mark him for what he is. Not that there is that in his countenance which Lombroso would have us believe signifies that he is a degenerate, congenitally deformed or insane, but rather that the life he leads gives him a look which the experienced observer knows as the "mug of a crook." He can no more change this look after reaching manhood than can a genuinely honest man, who has never been in prison, acquire it. I had learned to know it, and had become practiced in discovering it long before I became a policeman. It took me years to reach the stage when in merely looking hurriedly at a criminal something instinctively pronounced him to be a thief, but such a time certainly comes to him who sojourns much in criminal environment. There are, of course, certain special features and wrinkles that one looks for, and that help in the general summing up, but after a while these are not thought of in judging a man, at least not consciously, and the observer bases his opinion on instinctive feeling. Given the stylish clothes to which I have referred, a hard face, suspicious eyes which seem to take in everything, a loitering walk, a peculiar guttural cough given by way of signal, and called the thief's cough, and a habit of lingering about places where a "sporty" constituency is usually to be found, and there is pretty conclusive evidence that a professional thief is in view. All of this evidence is not always at hand; sometimes there is only the cough to go by, but the circumstances being suspicious any one of them is sufficient to make an expert observer look quickly and prick up his ears.

In New York City, for instance, there are streets in which professional thieves can be met by the dozen, if one understands how to identify them, and it is only necessary to pass a few words and they can be drawn into conversation. Some are dressed better than others—there are a great many ups and downs in the profession—and some look less typical than the more experienced men—it takes time for the life to leave its traces—but there they stand, the young and old, the clever and the stupid, for any one who knows how to scrape acquaintance with them. They are the most difficult people in the world to learn to know well until one has mastered their free masonry, and then they are but little more fearful of approach than is the tramp.

I devote a special chapter to their class because I believe that they are the least understood of all offenders, and also, as I stated above, because I consider them the real crux of the problem of crime in this country. The petty offender is comparatively easy to discourage, the backwoods criminal will disappear as our country develops, the born criminal, the man who says that he cannot help committing crimes, can be

shut up indefinitely, but the professional criminal seems to baffle the criminologist as well as the penologist, and he probably does more financial damage to the community than all the others put together. He is the man that we must apprehend and punish before crime in the United States will fail to be attractive, and at the present moment it is its attractiveness which helps to make our criminal statistics so alarming.

I have placed him third in numerical strength in my general classification, and I believe this to be a correct estimate of the number of those who really make their living by professional thieving, but it is thought by many, who do not discriminate in this particular, that he leads in the general criminal population. If those are to be included who would like to succeed as professional thieves and fail, and drop down sooner or later into the occasional criminal's class, the position I have given the so-called successful "professional" would have to be changed; but it has seemed best to confine the class to those who are rated successful, and on this basis I doubt whether an actual census taking, if it were possible, would prove them to be more numerous than I have indicated. Seeing and hearing so much of them on my travels I made every effort to secure trustworthy statistics in regard to their number, and as the bulk of them are known to the police, it seemed reasonable to suppose that, if I passed round enough among different police organizations, I ought to get satisfactory figures, but the fact of the matter is that the police themselves can only make guesses concerning the general situation, and I am unable to do any better.

When putting queries concerning the number of the offenders in question, my informants wanted me to differentiate and ask them about particular kinds of professionals before they would reply. One very well informed detective, for instance, said: "Do you mean the whole push, or just the A No. 1 guns? If you mean the push, why you're safe in saying that there are 100,000 in the whole country, but the most of 'em are a pretty poor lot. If you mean the really good people, 10,000 will take 'em all in."

The cities which were reported to have

The Independent

OCTOBER 26, 1899

Ten Cents a Copy = Two Dollars a Year

130 FULTON STREET, NEW YORK

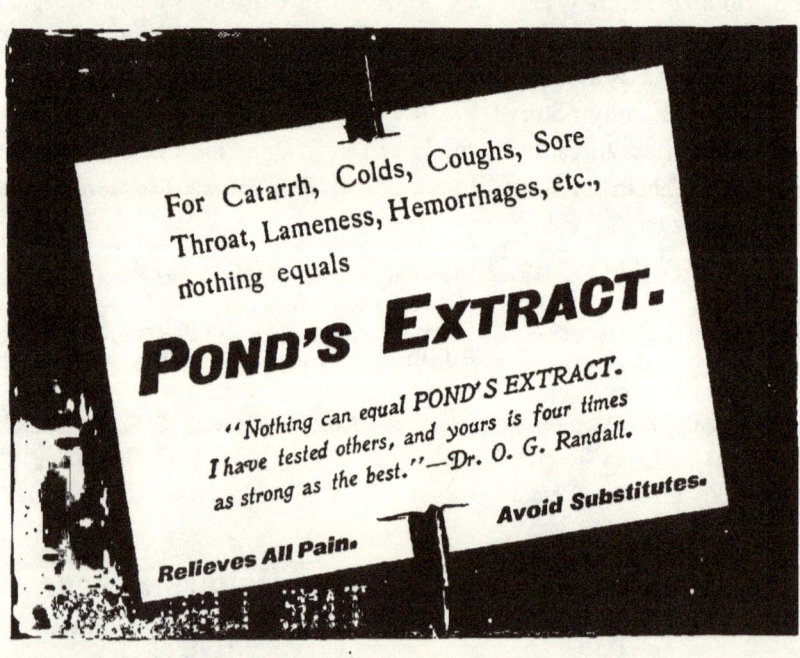

FIFTY-FOURTH ANNUAL STATEMENT
NEW=YORK LIFE INSURANCE COMPANY

Nos. 346 and 348 Broadway, New York City.

JOHN A. McCALL, - - - - **President.**

BALANCE SHEET, JANUARY 1ST, 1899.

ASSETS.

United States, State, City, County and other Bonds (cost value $115,687,034), market value, Dec. 31, 1898... $121,579,619
Bonds and Mortgages (777 first liens)........................ 39,002,758
Real Estate (68 pieces, including 12 office buildings)... 16,539,000
Deposits in Trust Companies and Banks, at interest ... 8,434,786
Loans to Policy-holders on their policies as security (legal value thereof, $16,000,000)...................... 9,818,600
Loans on Stocks and Bonds (market value, $9,229,702).. 7,390,845
Stocks of Banks, Trust Companies, &c. ($4,532,036 cost value), market value, Dec. 31, 1898........................ 6,050,831
Premiums in transit, reserve charged in Liabilities.... 2,280,188
Quarterly and Semi-Annual Premiums not yet due, reserve charged in Liabilities........................ 2,087,274
Interest and Rents due and accrued......................... 1,440,497
Premium Notes on policies in force (legal value of policies, $2,500,000......................... 1,820,423

TOTAL ASSETS.................. $215,944,811

LIABILITIES.

Policy Reserve (per certificate of New York Insurance Department............. $175,710,249
All other Liabilities: Policy Claims, Annuities, Endowments &c., awaiting presentment for payment......... 2,358,383 — $174,068,632
Additional Policy Reserve voluntarily set aside by the Company 2,888,626
Surplus Reserved Funds voluntarily set aside by the Company......................... 26,414,234
Other Funds for all other contingencies......................... 8,623,319 — 37,876,179

TOTAL LIABILITIES.................. $215,944,811

CASH INCOME, 1898.

New Premiums...............................$7,644,715
Renewal Premiums.......................27,987,933

TOTAL PREMIUMS..................$35,632,648

Interest on:
Bonds...........................$5,740,819
Mortgages........................1,940,937
Loans to Policy-holders, secured by reserves on policies................ 628,638
Other Securities....................... 391,353
Rents received........................... 875,741
Dividends on Stocks...................... 221,780

TOTAL, INTEREST, RENTS, &c...... 9,799,268

TOTAL INCOME........ $45,431,916

EXPENDITURES, 1898.

Paid for Losses, Endowments and Annuities... .. $15,390,978
Paid for Dividends and Surrender Values...... 6,124,883
Commissions ($3,320,904.33) on New Business of $152,098,369 ; Medical Examiners' Fees, and Inspection of Risks ($449,428)...................... 3,770,322
Home and Branch Office Expenses, Taxes, Advertising, Equipment Account, Telegraph, Postage, Commissions on $791,927,751 of Old Business and Miscellaneous Expenditures. 5,308,754
Balance—Excess of Income over Expenditures for year............................ 14,932,984

TOTAL EXPENDITURES..................$45,431,916

INSURANCE ACCOUNT.
ON THE BASIS OF PAID-FOR BUSINESS ONLY.

	NUMBER OF POLICIES.	AMOUNT.
In Force, December 31, 1897...	332,958	$877,020,925
New Insurance Paid-for, 1898...	73,471	152,098,369
Old Insurances revived and Increased, 1898..........	835	2,129,688
TOTAL PAID-FOR BUSINESS	407,264,	$1,031,243,982
DEDUCT TERMINATIONS: By Death, Maturity, Surrender, Expiry, &c.....	33,330	$87,222,862
Paid-for Business in Force December 31st, 1898........	**373,934**	**$944,021,120**
Gain in 1898.......................	40,976	$67,000,195
New Applications Declined in 1898	6,142	15,986,836

COMPARISON FOR SEVEN YEARS.
(1891-1898.)

	Dec. 31st, 1891.	Dec. 31st, 1898.	Gain in Seven Years.
Assets......	$125,947,290	$215,944,811	$89,997,521
Income.....	31,854,194	45,431,917	13,577,723
Dividends of Year to Policy Holders......	1,260,340	2,759,432	1,499,092
Total Payments of Year to Policy Holders......	12,671,491	21,519,865	8,848,374
Number of Policies in Force........	182,803	373,934	191,131
Insurance in Force, premiums paid......	$575,689,649	$944,021,120	$368,331,471

Certificate of Superintendent of State of New York Insurance Department.

ALBANY, January 6th, 1899.

I, LOUIS F. PAYN, Superintendent of Insurance of the State of New York, do hereby certify that the NEW-YORK LIFE INSURANCE COMPANY, of the City of New York, in the State of New York, is duly authorized to transact the business of Life Insurance in this State.

I FURTHER CERTIFY that, in accordance with the provisions of Section Eighty-four of the Insurance law of the State of New York, I have caused the policy obligations of the said company, outstanding on the 31st day of December, 1898, to be valued as per the Combined Experience Table of Mortality, at four per cent. interest, and I certify the same to be $175,710,249.

I FURTHER CERTIFY that the admitted assets are

$215,944,811.

THE GENERAL LIABILITIES, $2,358,383. THE NET POLICY RESERVE, AS CALCULATED BY THIS DEPARTMENT, $175,710,249, MAKING THE TOTAL LIABILITIES PER STATE LAWS,

$178,068,632.

THE ADDITIONAL POLICY RESERVE VOLUNTARILY SET ASIDE BY THE COMPANY,

$2,888,626.

THE SURPLUS RESERVED FUNDS VOLUNTARILY SET ASIDE BY THE COMPANY,

$26,414,234.

OTHER FUNDS FOR ALL OTHER CONTINGENCIES,

$8,623,819.

IN WITNESS WHEREOF, I have hereunto subscribed my name and caused my official seal to be affixed at the City of Albany, the day and year first above written.

LOUIS F. PAYN,
~SUPERINTENDENT OF INSURANCE

T H E

A L A S K A   B O U N D A R Y   L I N E

BY

THOMAS CORWIN MENDENHALL

with map

BULLETIN

OF THE

AMERICAN GEOGRAPHICAL SOCIETY

1 9 0 0

SKETCH-MAP OF SOUTH-EAST ALASKA.

THE ALASKA BOUNDARY LINE,

AN ADDRESS BEFORE THE AMERICAN GEOGRAPHICAL SOCIETY,

BY

T. C. MENDENHALL,

President of the Worcester Polytechnic Institute.

A few years ago I had the pleasure of addressing the Society upon the Boundary Line separating Southeast Alaska from the British Northwest Territory, calling attention to the ambiguous and uncertain definition of the line in the treaty between Russia and Great Britain, in which it was originally defined, and predicting a controversy, the beginnings of which were even then in evidence. Since then, as everybody knows, this controversy has grown in magnitude and intensity until it has attracted the attention of most intelligent people, and it is everywhere acknowledged to be of such importance as to justify a review of the situation at the present time. As a nation we have often been singularly negligent in the making of treaties involving delimitation of territory, and especially so in our intercourse with Great Britain, with which nation our territorial relations have been most intimate. Up to this time we have shown little, because we have felt little, of that spirit of "hold-fast," which has always characterized the diplomatic policy of the English people. We have been so busy in the occupation and development of the great interior that a few hundred square miles here and there of distant, unsettled regions have seemed to us of little importance. A better understanding on the part of the masses of our people of the interests involved would do much to secure a more vigorous support of just claims on the part of our government authorities; and it is hoped that a dissemination of better information as to the nature of the present dispute will result in a popular demand for a rigid insistence upon those claims. But it must not be assumed that the question of the Alaska Boundary is entirely one-sided. There are serious difficulties in the interpretation of the language of the treaty, and to some of these it will be well to give careful consideration.

It is well known that in the purchase of this territory in 1867 it was conveyed to us in the language of the treaty between Russia and Great Britain, made in 1825. Whatever jurisdiction and rights we may possibly claim now were those claimed and exercised by Russia from 1825 to 1867—no more and no less.

That part of the treaty which is responsible for the pending controversy is as follows:

" Commencing from the southernmost point of the Island called Prince of Wales Island, which point lies in the parallel of 54° 40′ north latitude and between the 131st and 133d degrees of west longitude (meridian of Greenwich), the said line shall ascend to the north along the channel called Portland Channel as far as the point of the continent where it strikes the 56th degree of north latitude ; from this last-mentioned point the line of demarcation shall follow the summit of the mountains situated parallel to the coast as far as the point of intersection of the 141st degree of west longitude (of the same meridian) and finally from the said point of intersection, the said meridian line of the 141st degree, in its prolongation as far as the frozen ocean."

The first apparent difficulty is the determination of what is meant by "the channel called Portland Channel." The Canadians, many of them, have interpreted this to mean that on leaving the southernmost point of Prince of Wales Island the line should be drawn at once to the north as far as the 56th parallel of north latitude, and this carries it to the west of the great Revilla Gigedo Island into Burrough's Bay,* thus throwing that island and a large block of the mainland under their jurisdiction, although now claimed by us. In order to enter what has always been known as Portland Channel it is necessary to proceed from the beginning at Prince of Wales Island straight to the east for about sixty miles, and then "ascend to the north along the channel," which is the line we claim. The omission of a reference to this easterly line in the treaty opens the door for the British contention, and to support it they maintain that the use of the name Portland Channel was an oversight. We contend, on the contrary, that the omission of the fifty or sixty miles of easting from the southernmost point of the Prince of Wales Island is of no special importance, because it would be assumed that before you can ascend along a channel you must get into it.

This point was strongly insisted upon for several years by Canadian authorities, but it has been practically given up as unreasonable and untenable, in the conferences of the Joint Commissioners appointed a year or two ago. A far more serious claim is based on the next phrase of the treaty, which declares that after leaving Portland Channel

" the line of demarcation shall follow the summit of the mountains situated parallel to the coast as far as the point of intersection of the 141st degree of west longitude," etc.

---

* Or Inlet.

The charts of this region on which the treaty-makers principally relied were those of Vancouver, who explored the northwest coast in the interests of the British Government about one hundred years ago. Vancouver traversed the estuaries and followed the windings of the coast pretty thoroughly, but he did not go inland, all of his work being done, in fact, from the deck of his ship. On his charts a beautifully continuous range of mountains is shown, skirting the coast about 35 miles back from the shore. This range was proposed by the Russian diplomats as a suitable natural boundary. The English, however, were suspicious of the accuracy of Vancouver's map, and were especially concerned lest the range of mountains shown thereon should be found to be really further from the coast than 10 marine leagues. They cited the fact that they had only a few years before encountered difficulty in settling a boundary controversy with the United States, on account of the discovery that mountain ranges shown upon the map did not so exist actually upon the ground. They proposed that the line should be fixed at ten marine leagues, about 35 miles, from the windings of the coast, and it was finally agreed to insert the modifying clause,

"that whenever the summit of the mountains which extend in a direction parallel to the coast from the 56th degree of north latitude to the point of intersection of the 141st degree of west longitude shall prove to be at a distance of more than ten marine leagues from the ocean, the limit between the British possessions and the line of coast which is to belong to Russia, as above mentioned, shall be formed by a line parallel to the winding of the coast, and which shall never exceed the distance of ten marine leagues therefrom."

It is a fact of the utmost importance that the English representatives were willing to accept a line "always at a distance of ten marine leagues from the shore," and that they protected themselves against a possible divergence of the supposed range of mountains to a greater distance inland. The extension of the line to the north along the 141st degree of longitude west of Greenwich is a simple astronomical problem over which there can be no dispute, and so the whole controversy is over the meaning of that part of the treaty which defines the boundary from the point where the Portland Channel meets the 56th parallel of north latitude to the 141st meridian, which it intersects very nearly at the summit of Mount St. Elias. The superiority of English diplomacy is shown in the wording of the treaty so that, while the swinging of the mountain range inland beyond the ten marine leagues shall not carry the boundary line with it, if it should be found to be really less than that distance from the shore, the Russian holdings must be reduced accordingly.

About ten years ago the United States began a survey for the purpose of definitely locating this boundary line. The first work was the establishment of astronomical stations on tributaries of the Yukon, to determine and mark at a few important points the 141st meridian north of Mount St. Elias. About 1891 a survey of the lower part of the region traversed by the boundary was undertaken by the United States and Canada jointly, but it was agreed that the two parties should work independently of each other, so that more ground might be covered, each Government to receive the results of the work of the other. A large part of the work was topographical, especially that of the Canadian parties.

The result of this survey was to prove, at least to the satisfaction of those representing the American side of the controversy, that the range of mountains shown on Vancouver's map does t exist, and that within the prescribed distance of ten marine leag es there is *no* range of mountains in Southeast Alaska "parallel to the windings of the coast." Mountains there are in plenty, but they are scattered about in absolute irregularity, generally increasing in height towards the east, but nowhere simulating a range, except in the northern extremity of the territory under consideration, where is to be found the Fairweather range, and possibly for a short distance in the neighborhood of the White and Chilkoot passes.

The American contention is, therefore, that in view of the failure of the first paragraph in its application to existing conditions, it becomes necessary to fall back upon the second and fix the boundary line at ten marine leagues from the shore, parallel to the windings of the coast.

To this argument Canadians have replied that the phrase "shall follow the summit of the mountains parallel to the coast" is applicable to those mountains which are admitted to be generally but irregularly distributed over the strip of territory in dispute, and that the line should be laid down by joining the summits of those nearest the shore. The effect of the adoption of this principle is to place the line everywhere very near the coast, leaving almost nothing but the western mountain slopes to the United States, and, what is more important, interrupting at several points the continuity of our coast line, giving to Great Britain many important estuaries, waterways and harbors. Indeed, it is clear in all of the negotiations that the primary object of Great Britain is to obtain coast line by which she may control admission to the interior.

Recognizing the difficulty of interpreting this treaty, Americans have very properly called to their support the doctrine of *vested rights*, accruing from continuous and undisputed and *unmixed* occupancy. Here it cannot be denied that everything is in our favor. From 1825 to 1867 the Russians claimed this territory, as we now claim it, without a word of protest from Great Britain. Not only Russian maps, but *all* maps drawn, up to a very recent time, showed the boundary where we believe it should be. All English charts so represent it. The Hudson Bay Company, an English corporation, leased from Russia a large part of this strip of land, following and adopting the boundary line as now claimed by us, paying an annual rental for its use. Before Parliamentary Committees the territory thus leased was defined and acknowledged by these maps, and in numerous proceedings the Russian claim was admitted without question. Many important points were actually occupied by Russian colonies, and none by British.

After the United States assumed jurisdiction in 1867, the Department of State published a map showing the bounds of the newly acquired territory; many American enterprises were established within the now disputed area, some at the extremest points, all without a word from Great Britain; and there was never an attempt to colonize this region by British subjects. Only a little more than ten years ago, when the value of the mineral resources of the region began to be understood, the first Canadian map was printed showing any other line than that now claimed by us. Even now English maps, almost without exception, show the boundary line as it is found on our own maps, and as late as about a year ago the *Scottish Geographical Magazine*, an acknowledged authority on cartography, published a very complete map of the whole region, with the boundary laid down in agreement with American claims. As to the absolute justice of these claims there can be no doubt in the minds of competent but unbiassed authorities. During the session of the Joint Commission the British Commissioners submitted a proposal to arbitrate the whole question in conformity to the terms of the Venezuelan arbitration, but they declined to consent to the selection of an umpire from the American continent. The American Commissioners proposed to submit the matter to a tribunal consisting of three judges of the highest standing in each country, a binding decision to be reached by at least four of these. This proposition, which must impress all as being eminently fair, was rejected by the British Commissioners, and no further attempt to reach an agreement was made by the Joint Commission.

Through the ordinary diplomatic channels a tentative agreement

has been reached, covering a small portion of the line in the neighborhood of the passes at the head of Lynn Canal, where most con-
flict of jurisdiction has occurred, and a temporary relief from
strained relations is promised.   It will be but temporary, however,
and it would have been safer and better if the United States had
stood squarely for its contention in every detail.   If once submitted to arbitration the result would be a compromise, regardless
of our real rights, and these are so clear that no concession ought
to be made.

www.ingramcontent.com/pod-product-compliance
Lightning Source LLC
Chambersburg PA
CBHW020707260626
47157CB00008B/3184